I0669772

Michael Arne, John Howkesworth

Edgar and Emmeline

A fairy tale, in a dramatic entertainment of two acts. As it is performed at

the Theatre-Royal in Drury-Lane

Michael Arne, John Howkesworth

Edgar and Emmeline
A fairy tale, in a dramatic entertainment of two acts. As it is performed at the Theatre-Royal in Drury-Lane

ISBN/EAN: 9783337245771

Printed in Europe, USA, Canada, Australia, Japan

Cover: Foto ©Andreas Hilbeck / pixelio.de

More available books at **www.hansebooks.com**

EDGAR and EMMELINE;

A

FAIRY TALE:

IN

A DRAMATIC ENTERTAINMENT

Of TWO ACTS;

As it is performed at

The THEATRE-ROYAL in DRURY-LANE.

LONDON,

Printed for H. PAYNE and W. CROPLEY, at Dryden's
Head, in Pater-noster Row.   1761.

Dramatis Personæ.

MEN.

EDGAR, son to the Earl of KENT, disguised as a Woman, under the name of ELFRIDA, } Mr. OBRIEN.

FLORIMOND, a Courtier,   Mr. KING.

WOMEN.

EMMELINE, daughter to the Earl of NORTHUMBERLAND, disguised as a Man, under the Name of GONDIBERT, } Mrs. YATES.

ELFINA, a Fairy,   Master KENNEDY.
GRUTILLA, a Fairy,   Miss ROGERS.
An attendant Fairy,   Miss WRIGHT.
Other Fairies, Servant, &c.

SCENE, Windsor-Castle, *and the Parts adjacent.*

The Music composed by Mr. ARNE, jun.

EDGAR and EMMELINE.

A

FAIRY TALE.

ACT I.

SCENE I.

A dark part of Windsor Forest; *the castle in prospect: one side of the horizon tinged with the rays of the setting sun; the moon rising on the other. Light music. Several fairies enter in grotesque characters, moving to the music, and at length forming a ring and dancing.*

Enter another FAIRY.

RECITATIVE.

NOW no more in dells we sleep;
Here our revels now we keep,
By the moon, our silver sun—
See, our sports are now begun!

AIR.

Welcome with thy lambent light,
Welcome, lovely queen of night!
To thy gentle reign belong,
Love, and mirth, and dance, and song.

War, and strife, and toil, and care,
Now their works of woe forbear:
Night shall now for day atone;
Give the night to joy alone!
[The fairy mixes with those that dance.

Enter ELFINA, *an old fairy.*

Elf. Hift---break off!---My charge receive;
Then renew the fports ye leave.

  [*They leave off dancing*; *the mufic ceafes*; *and*
    Elfina *beckons firft one, then another, fpeaking*
    to them feparately.

When the midnight hour is nigh,
Duteous to your tafks apply.

You, the mifer's haunt be near;
Break his reft with caufelefs fear,
Creak his doors, his windows fhake,
'Till his iron heart fhall quake.

You, as gouty humours flow,
Pinch the glutton by the toe.

You, with boding dreams moleft
Proud ambition's anxious breaft.

You, with fancied ghofts affright
Atheifts in their own defpight:
Bold by day, the bluft'ring fpark
Turns believer in the dark.

Hence—of vice to work the woe,
And the weal of virtue, go!---

The fairies go out at one door; and as Elfina
is going out at the other,

Enter GROTILLA, *another old fairy.*

Grot. Sifter! fifter!
Elf. Whence com'ft thou?
Grot. I come far.
Elf. What to do? Tell me---
Grot. To confer with you.

Elf.

Elf. Yonder,—(*pointing to the castle*)
Grot. What ?
Elf. The castle there---
Grot. Well---
Elf. Contains my present care.
Grot. Briefly then thy care unfold.
Elf. Mark ! it shall be briefly told.
    Edgar, Emmeline, you knew---
Grot. Youthful both, and fair and true.
Elf. Thus their destiny was read,
    While the sisters spun their thread :

" This youth a maid, this maid a youth must find,
" The best, the fairest, both in form and mind :
" Each, as a friend, must each esteem, admire ;
" Yet catch no spark of amorous desire !
" Till this be done, no chance shall bliss bestow ;
" When this is done, no chance shall work them woe!

Grot. This was publish'd at their birth.
Elf. Right ; and well 'tis known on earth.
Grot. Blest I wish them—
Elf. So do I.
Grot. Can you help them—
Elf. Certainly.
Grot. Search the island round and round,
    None like either can be found.
Elf. Each by each must then be seen ;
    But not lov'd---
Grot. Hard task, I ween !
Elf. Hard the task, I know it well.
Grot. How perform it ?—
Elf. I can tell.
    Here the king pursues the chace ;
    All his nobles crowd the place :
    Emm'line here a youth appears,
    Gondibert the name she bears ;

Edgar

Edgar is a maid in drefs,
Call'd *Elfrida*---

Grot. Now I guefs.

Elf. To the youth, the virgin feems,
Like himfelf, a youth; and deems,
Like herfelf, the youth a maid;
Neither thus to love betray'd.

Grot. You contriv'd---

Elf. I did---

Grot. But---

Elf. Stay!
Mortal footfteps mark the way.
Vanifh---quick! and leave me here:
If conjur'd, I muft appear.

[*Exit* Grotilla; Elfina *retires.*

Enter EMMELINE, *difguifed in a man's habit,
as* GONDIBERT.

Emm. What a fituation am I in !----Is this figure
really and truly *Emmeline* — the beloved and only
daughter of great *Northumberland?* Every thing
about me is fo like a dream, that I am frighted to
think I am awake.——O how weary I am of this drefs !
If I had known half that I fhould have fuffered in it,
all the fairies in the world fhould not have perfuaded
me to put it on.----If I refided here in this difguife the month of the king's hunting, I was to
break the fpell I was born under, and my life was to
be happy----fo the fairy told me !——Yet the time ex-
pires to-morrow, and nothing has happened to me but
vexation and difappointment. I muft once more fee
this powerful yet decrepit being, who, though in-
vifible, is always within my call.----This ring, which
fhe gave me, convenes her: if I take it off and touch
it thrice, fhe appears——Once—twice—thrice !

[Elfina *comes forward, and touches her.*
Emm.

Emm. O fairy! my fituation is fuch as I can bear no longer.

Elf. Patience; for it ends to-morrow.

Emm. To-morrow!——to-morrow is a thoufand years—When the horfe has all he can bear, a feather will break his back.

Elf. What's the matter?

Emm. Matter! why, in the firft place, I have lived almoft a month in a court——

Elf. That your forrow?

Emm. That my forrow! yes—I that have always lived in my father's principality, fair *Northumberland*, where a noble fimplicity of manners fhewed the heart to be open and undefigning; have, by your perfuafion and affiftance, left it for a place, where hypocrify is avowed by the name of good breeding; where the moft fhameful licentioufnefs is juftified as gallantry; diffi-mulation and perfidy, as addrefs and good manage-ment; where felf-intereft is profeffed as the firft prin-ciple of wifdom, and virtue and public fpirit derided as extravagance and fuperftition.

Elf. But your drefs was your defence.

Emm. O! it is my drefs that expofes me to more than half that I fuffer. When one of my own fex is in company, I am comparatively happy; but how unfit for a woman's ear is the converfation of men, when it is not reftrained by knowing that a woman is prefent! I begin to fear that I fhould not have thought fo well even of thofe men I have been ufed to con-verfe with, if they had appeared to me as they appear to each other.——The friendfhip and confidence of thefe lords of the creation, have almoft robbed me, a weak woman, of my allegiance:——I am frighted at the thought of living among them.

Elf. Fear not vices you deteft.

Emm. Fear not! but what muft I hope? O fairy! if I have implicitly followed your inftructions, if I have hidden them in my breaft from every friend,

and

and even from good *Northumberland* my father, let me no longer suffer the anguish of suspense.

Elf. Persevere; believe; confide.

Emm. But I have yet found no object worthy of my love.

Elf. You must find, and know it not.
Such the Fates ordain'd thy lot!

Emm. I know the mystery of my fate—that the happiness of my life depends upon my seeing and making a friend of the most beautiful and accomplish'd of men, without one thought of love—Alas!—forgive my doubts, my fears—should you——

Elf. Hold! of foul mistrust beware——To morrow!..——

Emm. Well then, till to-morrow—

Elf. Soft—unhallowed feet are nigh!—*Florimond*—

Emm. O! that wretch haunts me like my shadow. To rally me for what he calls my virtue, seems to be his supreme delight; he is proud of his own insensibility to what gives me pain: the confusion he throws me into, he considers as a test of his own abilities and accomplishments; and as vanity is his predominant passion, he is so assiduous to secure the enjoyment of his superiority, that I can scarce escape him one hour in a day.

Elf. He shall work thee woe and weal,
As to-morrow shall reveal.

Emm. But how? where?—dear, dear fairy!—

Elf. Ha, ha, ha! How and where must still perplex ye;
And, in kindness, I must vex ye—Ha, ha, ha!

[Elfina *disappears.*

Emm. Gone!—Mystery! perplexity, and distress! She sports too with my anxiety! I almost wish I had not trusted her: but 'tis too late—Here comes *Florimond*, and my torment begins.

Enter

Enter FLORIMOND, *singing.*

Flor. Ha! my little *Gondibertus!* have I found you?—What all alone *(peeping about)*? Egad I was in hopes there had been a wench in the cafe, and that I might have given thee joy of thy reformation.

Emm. Sir, I chofe to be alone. Solitude is fome-times not only ufeful, but pleafant.

Flor. Why 'tis a fine moon-light evening indeed—But what the devil—

Emm. I have fufficient fubject for meditation, Sir; and I hoped that, as there is a ball at the caftle to-night, you would have been better engag'd than to watch my privacy.

Flor. What! better engag'd than to raife fuch a re-cruit for the beau monde, as thou art?—Come, come, thou fhalt not thus fteal away from good company to thyfelf.

Emm. Sir, upon my word, I'm fit company for none but myfelf at prefent.

Flor. Pfhaw!—what always muzzy, with a difmal countenance as long as a taylor's bill! Come, chear up, boy, I've news for thee.

Emm. For me, Sir! *(alarm'd)*

Flor. Aye, to divert thee I mean; that's all.

Emm. What, is it any thing uncommon then?

Flor. No faith, not very uncommon neither; tho' perhaps thou may'ft make a wonder of it.—'Tis only an heirefs that's juft run away with a young fellow.

Emm. That, indeed, is not fo uncommon as might be wifh'd. But who is fhe? is fhe of any fafhion?

Flor. Yes faith, fhe is of fome fafhion; *Northum-berland's* fair daughter *Emmeline*, that's all—

Emm. Oh!—

Flor. What, thy virtue is fhock'd at the licent'ouf-nefs of the age? Ha, ha, ha!—Or art thou a lover of the fair *Emmeline's?* hey!

Emm.

Emm. (*aside.*) What shall I say? my confusion will certainly betray me—'Twas only a sudden pain shot cross my breast—But what particulars do you hear?

Flor. Why it seems she got leave of her father to follow him hither; and it is just accidentally discovered, that she left his castle the next day, though she has not been here yet.

Emm. Well; but why do you therefore conclude, that she's gone off with a man?.

Flor. Why only because the duke of *Kent*'s son, *Edgar*, disappeared upon the same pretence, just at the same time; and both have been missing ever since.

Emm. And is this sufficient to authorize a positive assertion to the prejudice of a reputation, which hitherto not slander itself has presum'd to stain?

Flor. Ha! ha! ha! Not slander itself has presum'd to stain! Ha, ha, ha. (*Mimicking her.*)

Emm. (*aside.*) O my heart! what new insult am I doom'd to suffer?—You'll excuse me, Sir, if, upon this occasion, I take the liberty to tell you, that your mirth is rather ill-timed; and—

Flor. Sir—do you know this fair lady, that you are so much disposed to become her knight-errant?

Emm. (*aside.*) I must be cautious, or my zeal may discover me. Sir, though I should not know her, it is my point of honour, never to suffer the reputation of the absent to be wantonly sported away, upon mere circumstances and surmise.

Flor. Your point of honour!—why to be sure all this is very fine. But I'll tell you a secret, my dear—As unstain'd as you may think the fair *Emmeline*'s reputation, there is a certain humble servant of yours, that shall be nameless, who has some *small* reason to think, that a certain piece of brittle ware, which she had the keeping of, may be a little crack'd—or so.

Emm. (*aside*) A wretch! who never saw me but in this disguise—You are well acquainted with her then?

Flor. Why—I am—

Emm.

Emm. And pray, what kind of woman is she?

Flor. Why, she's a pretty—upon my word, a very pretty wench.

Emm. But is she tall, or short, or brown, or fair?

Flor. You have never seen her, you say?

Emm. No more than I do this moment.

Flor. (aside.) Then I may venture—Why she is fair, tall, and slender; has a fine neck, a very fine neck! her limbs remarkably well turn'd, her leg and ancle the finest I ever saw—

Emm. (distress'd and confounded.) Oh!

Flor. Aye—I thought I should set you a longing: but come, she's not to be had at present it seems; so no more of her.

Emm. I cannot so easily dismiss her as you may imagine; and yet, perhaps, you may mistake the reason.

Flor. Very likely, faith; but what is it?

Emm. Why I am astonish'd, that you make so light of what has happen'd to her; whether you consider it as the loss of a mistress, or whether as a misfortune to a woman you must be suppos'd to have lov'd, and to whom you must have had obligations of the strongest and most tender kind: one of these lights you must see it in.

Flor. Why, my dear, as to that, I am extreamly easy about losing her; for between you and I—I cou'd spare her. I must, indeed, confess, that I was very fond of her once; but 'faith, the obligations were all on her side—It's among ourselves.

Emm. (aside) O, my heart! what a monstrous compound of vanity and lies is this!—How so, pray sir?

Flor. Why, I us'd to meet her in her father's park night after night, at the risk of my life; and egad, what with the danger, and what with the fatigue, I grew tir'd of her; and, to tell you the truth, provided her another lover, to make good my retreat. It's among ourselves.

C   *Emm.*

Emm. Well faid—and who was that, fir ?

Flor. The very fame *Edgar* that fhe is now run away with. I thought it would be a pretty thing for him ; for he is one of your fighting fellows, that is never fo happy as when he's in danger—but I'm forry he has been fo indifcreet.

Emm. Pray, Sir—excufe me—I don't pretend to queftion the truth of what you fay ; but there are fome difficulties in the ftory, that I fhould be glad to have clear'd up—If you was fo much in the lady *Emmeline's* good graces, and had, as you fay, no diflike to her perfon, how came you not to think of marrying her ? Such an alliance, I prefume, would not have difhonoured you.—I fhall confound him now.   [*Afide.*

Flor. Marrying her! Egad, fhe knew a trick worth two o'that. I would have married her ; and I told her fo : " My dear *Florimond*," fays fhe,—her arm was then lying negligently crofs my fhoulder, thus,---and fhe look'd archly at me, thus,---" My dear *Flo-*
" *rimond*," fays fhe, " why fhould you and I, that
" have now only the power of making each other
" happy, fuffer a doating old prieft to give us the
" power of making each other miferable ? If you
" were to be my hufband, you might ceafe to be my
" lover ; and then," fays fhe, with a moft roguifh
leer, " perhaps I might be tempted to take another :
" you would tyrannize, I fhould rebel ; you wou'd
" enjoy nothing but the hope of breaking my heart,
" and I fhould enjoy nothing but the hope of break-
" ing yours."

Emm. (*afide.*) Still, ftill, I draw upon myfelf more confufion.—But why then did fhe run away with *Edgar?* That muft ruin her fchemes, both of intereft and pleafure.

Flor. Nay, how the devil can I tell that ?

        [Emmeline *walks apart, confus'd and embarrafs'd*
                                         Flor.

Flor. What, in your reveries !----Thou art now mufing on fome *vartuous* love, like an ever faithful *lowyer tell* death,---ha, ha, ha !---Come, come, pfhaw, don't be a fool ; fome kind wench now would cure you----Egad, what think you of *Elfrida?*----Come along, we'll call at her apartment: perhaps fhe's dreffing, and we fhall be admitted to her toilet. Upon my foul, a fine figure of a woman ! a little mafculine, that's all ; but take my word for it, a delicious morfel for all that !---Hark ye--,if you are not fheepifh, fhe'll not be coy : it's among ourfelves---I tell you, as a friend ; 'faith I don't love to monopolize --I'll juft tickle up her fancy a little, and leave you together. Come---

Emm. Pray, fir---

Flor. I will, 'faith.

Emm. I muft infift---

Flor. Nay, nay, come along, come along.

[*Lays hold of her.*

Emm. Sir, I muft abfolutely be excus'd at prefent.

Flor. Why, what a plague is it now that thou haft taken into thy head ?

Emm. Sir, I have an affair that at prefent requires me to be alone ; which I cannot farther explain, than---

Flor. Say no more, fay no more. (*afide.*) Egad, I have guefs'd it now---A challenge !---why, there's light enough for two people to cut one another's throats by, to be fure---I'll away---Well, my dear, if I muft leave you to the dew and the moonfhine, I muft ; but d'ye hear---'faith I'll to *Elfrida*---will you follow me ? If you don't ftay too long, you'll find an *attendriffement*, that you may be oblig'd to your humble fervant for ; that's all---it's among ourfelves. ---Adieu. [*Exit.*

Emm. Why, fare thee well, thou---wretch, without a name----What will, what can become of me ?

C 2 What

What is it that prompts this fool, whom as I never knew, I never could provoke, to wrong me thus? is it a sacrifice to his vanity? or is it mere wantonness and sport?----Pray heav'n this fairy don't deceive me! ---What shall I do?---I must see her, and take her counsel in this new distress.

[*She takes off her ring, and touches it thrice; but the fairy does not appear.*

Ha!---sure I dream!--Forlorn, deserted!---this perfidious goblin!----Again I touch it; once---and twice ---and thrice--and yet she is not here!---O I could--- But though I see her not, she may be near me, to hear and punish the complaints which her unkindness forces from me---To whom can I now ease my heart!---O! sacred friendship!---but here I have no friend. *Elfrida* --yes, she indeed, as if by some secret sympathy, claims my confidence; and my heart tells me, she deserves it----Yes, I will trust her with my secret: she will be a witness for me against this slander, and assist me with her advice. [*Exit.*

[*The scene changes to* Edgar's *apartment, and discovers him at a toilet, dressing in the character of* Elfrida; *a woman attending.*

Edgar. Here, give me the ribbons.—Get you gone—I'll call you, when I want you.

Woman. (*aside*) This lady has the strangest humours!
[*Exit.*

Edgar. Was ever man in such ridiculous distress! I'm sure I ne'er knew any thing like it, since I was *Edgar* the son of *Kent.* Here have I had a young tempting girl fiddle-faddling about me these two hours to dress me, forsooth—with an officious handiness so provoking, that no virtue under that of a stockfish could endure it patiently. Yet an old woman upon these occasions I cannot bear; and, in short, I can no
longer

longer bear a young one —It is my fate, they fay, to be miferable, if I don't get acquainted with the fineft girl in *England*, without wifhing for her ; and I was told by a little goblin that ftarted up before me, after it had led me, under the appearance of a Jack o' Lantern, into a wood, That if I could fpend the king's hunting month here in this difguife, all would be right: but how my being in petticoats fhould make me lefs likely to love a fine girl, I cannot conceive ! A fine girl, indeed, may be lefs likely to love me ; but as to myfelf, it is high time for me to get into breeches, that I may get out of temptation. Here they flock about me—one fits down, juft before me, and, without any ceremony, ties her garter—another gets me to adjuft her tucker.—I'm the witnefs of fo many pranks, and the confidant of fo many fecrets! Then I have my hours of mortification too : I am tormented by a fwarm of profligate fops, who try to debauch every woman they fee, with as little concern as they take fnuff: wretches, who are as deftitute of love, as they are of virtue ; and have as little enjoy-ment, as they have underftanding ! And here I'm ob-liged to mince, and pifh, and 'fye,—and affect to blufh,—'sdeath, when I'm burfting with indignation, and long to knock 'em down—I'll bear it no longer.

ELFINA *fuddenly appears from under the toilet, and places herfelf before him.*

Edgar. Ha! What again ?

Elf. Again.

Edgar. Art thou my good or evil genius ? Tell me.

Elf. As you think me, you fhall find me.

Edgar. I will think thee then my good genius, for I would fain find thee fo.

Elf. You muft truft me too, or elfe---

Edgar. Truft you !—Look at the figure I make here, and then judge if I have not trufted you.

Elf. But your virtue muſt be tried.

Edgar. Tried!—By what new torments would you try it? Have I not ſuffered the two worſt things in nature, temptation and ſuſpenſe? Have not I——

Elf. No---you have not perſevered: all is loſt, if you give out.

Edgar. Reſolve my doubts then; torment me no longer with ſuſpenſe: let me be certain of the event, and I will be an anchorite, in ſpight of this habit and all its works, a month longer.

Elf. Well—Obſerve me then, and learn.

Edgar. (*eagerly*) What ſhall I learn?

Elf. Patience, *Edgar*!—Fare thee well. Ha, ha, ha! [*A machine riſes under her, and carries her away.*

Edgar. Derided, and forſaken!-----I doubt this is one of the wanton and miſchievous elves, that tantalize poor mortals for their own diverſion: however, as I have played in the farce ſo long, I'll not ſtop in the laſt ſcene.----

Enter Woman.

Woman. Ma'am, here's my lord *Trifle* has ſent his compliments to your la'aſhip; and begs to know, whether he ſhall have the honour of waiting upon your la'aſhip to the ball.

Edgar. (*recovering his female attitude, and accent*) My compliments, am much oblig'd to his lordſhip, but am engag'd.

Woman. Yes, ma'am.

Edgar. Harkye----

Woman. Ma'am.

Edgar. Has *Gondibert* call'd here this evening?

Woman. No, ma'am.

Edgar. Nor ſent?

Woman. No, ma'am. [*Exit.*

Edgar. There's a man, now, who might atone for the vices of the whole ſex! I am ſo anxious to recommend

mend myfelf to him, even in this difguife ; and feel
fuch a reluctance to do any thing that may difguft him,
even while he thinks me a woman ; that when he is
prefent, I labour to make my manner fuit with my
appearance, I know not how, by a kind of involun-
tary effort. How ftrange is the rapidity with which
fome minds unite !

Enter Woman.

Woman. Ma'am, there's count *Florimond.*
Edgar. Did not I tell you-----
Woman. Yes, ma'am ; and I told him,-----but he
faid he knew your la'afhip was at home, and that he
muft fee you.
Edgar. Muft fee me !
Woman. Yes, ma'am ; and though I told him your
la'afhip was a-dreffing, yet he would follow me.----O
Lord, he's the ftrangeft man !----He's here, an pleafe
your la'afhip.----

Enter FLORIMOND.

Edgar. (*afide*) What a farce muft I now act ! Pray
heav'n it has not a tragical cataftrophe !
Flor. My dear goddefs !
Edgar. Lard, how can you be fo monftrous rude !---
burfting into one's dreffing-room----and putting one
into fuch flurries-----

[*He fumbles at pinning on a breaft-knot.*

Flor. That your heart beats in concert with mine.---
The dear toilet is not more the altar of beauty, than
of love.---Permit me the honour, ma'am, of affifting
to place that envied ornament on your bofom.
Edgar. Lard, Sir !----I beg----not for the world---
you quite confound me----

Flor.

Flor. (pressing) My life! My angel!—

 [*Catches him hastily round the waist, and endeavours to kiss him; upon which* Edgar *gives him a smart blow on the ear.*

Edgar. Nay then there is no expedient----
Flor. (retreating backward) Ma'am!----

[Edgar *stamps, and* Florimond *starts and retreats farther back; at the same time*

EMMELINE, *as* GONDIBERT, *appears at the door.*

Flor. I protest, ma'am,----- *(frighted)*
Edgar. (sternly) And I protest, Sir,----
Flor. Ma'am, I beg-- -
Edgar. And I beg, Sir,----
Flor. (turning and seeing Gondibert*)* O-------Ma'am, your most humble servant.   [*going.*

Emm. (aside to Flor.*)* Sir-----I am under very great obligations to you----but I would not have you tickle up her fancy any more, upon my account-----
Flor. Duce take you!-----I wish you had been as near her as I was.

[*Is going, but again stops and adjusts his wig by a pocket mirrour.*

Edgar (to Emmeline, *recovering himself, and adjusting his dress)* Lord, Sir---I'm in such a flurry----I, I, I, I'm very sorry I should have been provok'd to any thing so unbecoming the delicacy of my sex.
Flor. Upon my soul, so am I too---------Sir, your humble servant.   [*Exit.*

Emm. You have no reason to apologize for your in-
dig-

dignation, madam; though your blow was something spirited, I must confess.

Edg. I'm in such confusion, sir—and he has made me such a figure!—to treat *me* with indecent familiarities!

Emm. Dear madam, compose yourself, and think no more of him. He has not been much better company to me, than he has to you, I'll assure you.

Edgar. Lord, sir, you surprise me!—Pray, what impertinence has he been guilty of to you?

Emm. He has been filling my ears with scandal, madam; a subject which seems to be equally suitable both to his abilities and disposition! He has been telling me, that *Edgar*—

Edgar. Who, sir? (*hastily.*)

Emm. *Edgar*, madam, the son of the earl of *Kent*—

Edgar. What of him, sir?—what scandal has he spread of *Edgar?*—

Emm. (*aside.*) Ha! so interested!—She loves him, sure.

Edgar. Let me conjure you, sir, if this wretch has said any thing to dishonour *Edgar*, you would tell it to *me.*

Emm. (*aside.*) It must be so—Your very earnestness forbids me, madam.

Edgar. I know I'm mov'd, and you must think it strange.

Emm. (*surpris'd at the masculine tone and manner into which his earnestness involuntarily betrays him*) Strange, indeed!—

Edgar. Perhaps, 'tis stranger still than you can think.

Emm. Your manner, madam—

Edgar. No matter — Forms and modes become trifles too small for notice, when they stand in competition with a friend's good name.

Emm. (*aside.*) Her love is to distraction—She frights me, and is not to be trusted—

D   *Edgar.*

Edgar. Let me conjure you—tell me—

Emm. I cannot tell you, madam.

Edgar. Cannot!

Emm. I ought not—Truft me there are reafons—Let it fuffice that in the ftory I have heard, a lady's honour is as much concern'd as *Edgar*'s; that the flander cannot intereft you, more than me; that I will do my utmoft to make it's falfehood fo notorious, that it cannot be believ'd; and I entreat that, as you tender your peace, you would as yet enquire no farther—I know myfelf not proof againft your importunity; and therefore you will excufe me, if, having no other way, I fave myfelf by flight.   [*Exit.*

[*Edgar runs out after her, but returns.*

Edgar. Curfe on this cumberfome habit! I cannot overtake him. Was ever any thing fo vexatious! I have been defam'd by fome fcandalous falfehood, and I muft do my honour juftice—I can, at a fmall expence of diffimulation, get that wretch, *Florimond*, to repeat to me all that he has told to *Gondibert*: I will do it—and I will as yet lie in ambufh under this difguife, to make fure of my blow.

[*Exit.*

EMMELINE, *as* GONDIBERT,
re-enters.

Emm. She's gone!—What can I, or what ought I to do? If I had told her the ftory, I muft have difcovered myfelf to convince her it could not be true: but who knows what a jealous woman might have thought upon finding the very perfon, who is faid to have gone off with her lover, in fo ftrange a difguife! —Yet fhe will certainly contrive to hear it from *Florimond*; and then, good heaven! what will fhe fuffer, if if I do not convince her that it is falfe!—I muft, I will truft her—I have no other chance to fave her, but by making a difcovery, which, if I had really gone off with *Edgar*, it is certain I fhould not have made, efpecially to her. But I muft not intrude upon her now: I will plant myfelf where I may intercept her before fhe can fee *Florimond*, and truft to generous friendfhip for the event. [*Exit.*

END of the FIRST ACT.

ACT

ACT II.

SCENE I.

The Terrace at Windſor Caſtle.

Enter FLORIMOND, *with a Letter.*

Flor. AYE---ſhe was obliged to be angry, be-
cauſe that fool *Gondibert* appear'd juſt
in the critical minute at the door---pox take him !---I
might have known it was not natural, by her over-
doing it---it was, indeed, overdone with a vengeance !
But now ſhe's in the pannicks, leſt 1 ſhould reſent it.
Now ſhe has ſomething to ſay---and---if I am diſen-
gag'd,---ſhe will be glad to meet me upon the terrace.
If I ſhould humble her now, and not meet her---but
rhat would be cruel.   I will, however, take ſome ſtate
upon me---I will look a little formal ; it may ſave me
ſome trouble in my future advances.---Here ſhe comes.

Enter EDGAR, *ſtill diſguis'd as* ELFRIDA.

   [Florimond *receives him with an air of negligent*
     haughtineſs, and makes a formal bow.

   Edgar. Sir, I hope you will not take any advantage
of my weakneſs---

   Flor. (*turning from her.*) Weakneſs ! pox on you---
Your weakneſs don't lie in your arm, I'm ſure o'that.

   Edgar. (*following.*) Or ſuppoſe, ſir, that whatever
reaſon I may have for deſiring this meeting---What
airs the wretch gives himſelf! (*aſide*)---I ſay, ſir, that
you would not ſuppoſe---I cannot contain myſelf !---
                                     [*Aſide.*

Flor. Poor foul! what confufion! I will relax a little of my feverity. (*Afide.*) Madam, I will fuppofe nothing, but that you have given me another opportunity of hearing your commands.

Edgar. I think, fir, you was telling *Gondibert* a certain affair between you, and *Edgar*, and a lady; and fomething that, by his manner of telling it, I could not very well underftand.

Flor. (*afide.*) Aye---a very good introduction---a love-ftory is a moft excellent prelude to a love-fcene--- I perceive we are to adjourn---Why, madam, a certain fair lady, call'd *Emmeline*, has thought fit to make *Edgar* as happy, as any man can be made, except him, madam, whom you fhall pleafe to honour with the fame favour---Upon my foul, fhe's a fine creature!

Edgar. Sir, your compliments really put me fo out of countenance---that I fhall blufh to death---

Flor. Your blufhes are fo becoming, madam, that---

Edgar. Give me leave, fir, to entreat, that you would at prefent fpare my confufion, and tell me all the particulars of that affair which have come to your knowledge.

Flor. Aye----fhe wants a lufcious defcription now. (*Afide.*) Why, madam, I prefume that *Edgar*, being fir'd with the charms of *Emmeline*, firft gaz'd languifhingly upon her; caught her eyes the firft time they were cafually turn'd upon him; when, in a foft confufion, fhe haftily turn'd her look downward and blufh'd; he took her hand, firft preffing it gently in his own, then raifing it to his lips; then, madam, I prefume he might proceed to---

Edgar. Sir!---I fhall certainly be out of patience, and knock him down (*afide.*)---Sir, if you have any defire to oblige me---or have any expectations, fir, of favours---Not, fir, that I---

Flor. My dear angel, keep me no longer in fufpenfe; let me know your commands, that I may fulfil the condition of--- [*Preffing. Edgar.*

Edgar. (*drawing back*) Hold, Sir---You muft then, without farther delay or interruption, give me a direct anfwer to a few fhort queftions.

Flor. Why, madam, it fhall then be in your own way.

Edgar. Firft then, Sir, are you acquainted with *Edgar,* the young heir of *Kent?*

Flor. Why, madam, to proceed implicitly as you direct, I believe there are few perfons who know more of that gentleman, than your humble fervant.

Edgar. (*afide*) Matchlefs impudence!——And pray, Sir, what kind of a youth is he?

Flor. (*afide*) I fee by her curiofity fhe don't know him——Why, madam, the youth is a, a, a, rather foft—a green youth, madam, as we fay——

Edgar. Sir, thefe are terms that I do not perfectly comprehend: and, therefore, I beg you would be more explicit.

Flor. Why then, explicitly, madam, he is, upon my foul, a fhallow fellow----a very fhallow fellow, faith---It's among ourfelves.

Edgar. He is.

Flor. He is indeed, madam.----The poor devil has fome aukward good nature, and I have a kindnefs for him; but, between you and I, he'll never be fo much a man of honour as 1 could wifh him----

Edgar. (*forgetting his feminine character, and running up to him*) How, villain!---

Flor. (*frighted and drawing back*) Ma'am-----!

Edgar. (*afide*) What have I done! (*he draws himfelf again into form*) To think of villainy in people that, by their rank, are fet up as examples to others, quite tranfports me out of myfelf.—Heigh ho!—It has quite overcome me.

[*Affects to be faint, and takes out a fmelling bottle.*

Flor. (*afide*) What a terrible virago it is!—May I prefume, madam, to lend you my hand.

[*approaching cautioufly.*

Edgar. It is over, Sir——I'm fo fubject to flur-ries----and my poor nerves are fo fhattered.—- I'm extremely obliged to you for this character of *Edgar*— To have been guilty of any thing bafe!---

Flor. Very bafe, I affure you, madam.

Edgar. Sir.--- (*affuming a fierce mafculine air, but inftantly correcting himfelf*)

Flor. Ma'am——(*ftarting back*) · Fore Gad, fhe's mad!--- and upon my foul in my opinion damnably mifchievous. (*afide*)—

Edgar. Give me leave, fir---as well as I am able---to afk you what in particular has—but I fee company coming ---If we walk this way, we fhall avoid them.

Flor. (*afide*) Avoid them!—Heaven forbid!—Perhaps, madam, another time—

Edgar. Sir, I fhall die, if my curiofity is not gratified.

Flor. Madam---at prefent I am---·

Edgar. Sir, I beg---for my reputation, that we may not be furpriz'd together, while I am in this diforder.

Flor. By no means, madam—let us part this mo-ment—If you'll go off one way, I'll go the other.

Edgar. O not for the world!—To be feen to part haftily, upon being obferved together, would be the fubject of eternal fcandal.——Let me beg the favour of your arm— (*lays hold of his arm*)

Flor. (*crying out*) Lard Gad, madam!—

Edgar. Sir?—

Flor. You'll pinch it through- --

Edgar. Lord, Sir, 'tis my fright——One naturally clafps any thing hard in a fright.

Flor. Madam, you do me honour—

[*Edgar holds his arm; he keeps as far off as he can, and fixes his eyes upon him, as they go out.*

By the heavens! fhe has the gripe of a bum-bailiff. (*afide.*) [*Exeunt.*

SCENE,

SCENE, *the dark Grove.*

Enter ELFINA.

Elf. Sifter! fifter!   (Grotilla *fuddenly appears*)
Grot. ————Here am I.
Elf. Now the fated hour is nigh
Keep the lovers in your eye.
Each to each fhall foon be known ;
Each for each was born alone.
Grot. Florimond, the caitiff vile---
Elf. They fhall profper by his guile :
(Evil we for good permit)
This their friendfhip's knot fhall knit.
But the fated hour is nigh----

Come, ye elves, whofe minds perceive,
    By fecret impulfe, what I will ;
Come, your fports this moment leave,
    And what I ordain fulfil.

                    [*Many fairies fuddenly appear.*

Now the fated hour is nigh,
To rites that charm from ill apply.
Form the circle on the dew,   (*they form a ring.*)
Round, and round, the track renew ;----

                            [*they dance.*

Mark it thrice, and thrice again—
Join with me the magic ftrain.

SONG.

By the bat's nocturnal flight
O'er the fleeping plants and flow'rs ;
By the moon's inconftant light,
Potent fpell of midnight hours—

                                        By

By the ring of various dies,
Circling oft the silver ball;
By the genial mists that rise,
By the virgin dews that fall.----

By the meteor's gleamy spark,
Wand'ring o'er the reedy lake;
Stars that shoot athwart the dark,
Lights from polar skies that break.----

By Night, and all things that to Night pertain---
Ye rival powers, from adverse arts abstain!
Intrude not now my purpose to contest;
But let the pair that I would bless, be blest.

Elf. Cease, the fated hour is nigh!---
Cease, and to the castle fly!
Careful watch the great event,
Finish'd ere the day be spent.
        [*Fairies and the scene disappear together.*

Enter EMMELINE, *still disguised as*
        GONDIBERT.

Emm. She's gone out, and I have unfortunately
missed her----She is certainly got to *Florimond*----Ha!
yonder they are---Yes, it is certainly so---What violent emotion!----Now they move hastily forward----
Now she stops short----her gestures are scarce femi-
nine----Now she recovers herself---*Florimond* too seems
to be frighted out of his gallantry, and extremely
willing to put an end to the conversation----'Tis over!
he leaves her, and she comes this way.----Yes, I will
open my whole heart to her; not for my sake now,
but her own. Whatever are the first sallies of her
surprize and passion, she must at length feel and return my friendship.-----Here she comes: I must not
accost her too abruptly.   (*Retires to a little distance.*)
        E   *Enter*

Enter EDGAR *still as* ELFRIDA. *Seeing*
EMMELINE, *he stops short.*

Edgar. Ha! *Gondibert*----I know the generous reafon, now, of his referve. In this difguife, what could
my intereft in *Edgar* appear to him, but love!----and
if it had been fo, how muft I have been hurt by what
he had to tell me!----But he is not lefs interefted in
the lady----fo he faid----Sure then he is to *Emmeline*,
what he thought *Edgar* was to me!-----Let me then
repay his generous kindnefs; let me difcover, not only
what, but *who* I am, to convince him that the tale is
falfe, which, if true, muft deftroy his peace. (*Going
up to* Emmeline)-----You need not fhun me, fir; I
have now nothing to afk, that you would wifh to conceal: I have only to requeft, that you would forgive
me for having violated your injunction, not to fatisfy
the curiofity you had raifed. I am apprized of your
kind, your generous motive; and it has infpired my
breaft with all that it is poffible I fhould feel for you,
a grateful and ardent friendfhip.

Emm. Your love, madam, I make no doubt, is
fixed on a much nobler and more deferving object.—
Edgar, I prefume----

Edgar. My connection with *Edgar*, fir, is indeed,
in fome fenfe, the reafon why your merit cannot make
an impreffion, which I am not afhamed to fay it might
otherwife have done: and yet, fir, let me confefs that
I am not affected by the ftory of his difappearing
with *Emmeline*, as you might reafonably imagine, becaufe I know for *certain* that it *cannot* be true.

Emm. (*haftily*) Ha! that it cannot be true---

Edgar. I now owe *your friendfhip* a difcovery, if indeed it is a difcovery, which I was prompted by mere
regard to myfelf to have made before: I think there is
a connection between you and *Emmeline*, that—

Emm.

Emm. There is, indeed, a connection, madam---a secret, which you convince me it is now in vain to affect to hide ---

Edgar. Let me then claim it—But let me first, as a pledge of that friendship which I hope shall end but with our lives, give, for your secret, mine.—

Emm. Do then, nor keep me longer in suspense; for still, the more we talk, the more I am perplexed. (*aside*) What can *her* secret be!

Edgar. Why then, in the first place, sir,---I am— a man --

Emm. (*aside, with great emotion, which she labours to conceal*) A man!—Good Heav'n! what will become of me!

Edgar. And now, let me at once embrace you as a friend: punctilios and forms no longer part us—

> [*As* Edgar *advances eagerly to* Emmeline, *she hides her face, and appears in great confusion.*

Edgar. (*hastily*) What ails my friend?

Emm. O! you have ruined all my pleasing project--- prevented—but no matter---

Edgar. This is amazing! For heaven's sake, what d'ye mean?—You was not sure enamoured of my person.---

Emm. O! no---You still mistake ---

Edgar. Then tell me my mistake; for we may now converse on even terms: our hearts may now be opened to each other, without the forms and the reserve prescribed in friendships with the softer sex.

Emm. O! still you wander, wide and wider still--- I cannot speak—

Edgar. You must---There is a secret, which, but now, your heart was ready to reveal---

Emm. And then I thought it known—but now—

Edgar. Now my warm heart has claimed you for my friend—

Emm.

Emm. And now to tell it is impoffible----I cannot tell it---and if I could, you would not find the friend-fhip that you hope——

⌊Edgar *looks earnestly at her, wond'ring and embarrass'd.*

(*afide*) I ficken at his fight----Oh my heart!

Edgar. I'm all perplexity and wonder!——Your co-lour comes and goes, like a fick girl's——(*She becomes more confused, as he marks her confusion*)——You trem-ble!—Heavens! he faints!----(*he catches her in his arms, and difcovers her breaft*) By all my wonder and my joy, a woman!----How lovely her confufion!——O let my bofom warm thee back to life! Look up, and truft the honour of my love: you fhall not whifper what you would conceal; nor will I feem to know it.

[*She recovers.*

Emm. O! let me hide me from myfelf---my fex thus known---in this difguife! Where fhall my con-fcious blufhes find a veil!---Who are you? Tell me, that I may hide me from your fight for ever.

Edgar. O! no---On that condition, let me ne'er be known.

Emm. Yet tell me---truft me---

Edgar. Truft thee! Yes, with my life I'd truft thee. Thy friend---O! know me by a fofter name--- is *Kent*'s young heir; that *Edgar* you have heard fo falfely and fo wantonly traduc'd.

Emm. Still wonders crowd on wonders!

Edgar. I dream myfelf, or this is all enchantment.

Emm. So might you think, indeed, if more you knew me.

Edgar. Let me then know thee more, whom now I know as the moft fair and gentle of thy fex; whom yet I faw and lov'd without defire----my pledge of happinefs!---May I be thine!---but yet I rave---thy fate was not like *Edgar*'s---

Emm.

Emm. Spare me—thy words have pow'r, which yet thou know'ft not.

Edgar. O! take me from the rack! My thoughts grow wild!---There is, indeed, a maid, whofe fate I've heard was fuch as mine---that *Emmeline*---O! heav'n, that *Emmeline*, in whom I thought thy intereft, love!----O! yes, it muft, it fhall----thou, thou art fhe!

Emm. Leave me, or I fhall die with my confufion---

Edgar. Let me fupport thee, hide thee in my breaft, where thou fhalt breathe thy anfwer in a figh.---Art thou not *Emmeline*, my fated love?

Emm. If *Emmeline* be thy fated love---I am---

Edgar. Still let me clafp thee clofe, and clofer ftill; calm all the tumults of thy feeling mind, and footh thee into confidence by love.

Emm. No, let me now retire: for, in this drefs, I cannot bear to fee myfelf, or you.

Edgar. Yet ftay—forgive the violence I do you— My fame and yours are wantonly traduc'd; 'tis fit that we do juftice to them both, and punifh the traducer.

Emm. He is not worth refentment.

Edgar. He is for others fakes, though not his own. ---I have a thought, would *Emmeline* but join—

Emm. Tell me then quickly.

Edgar. Send him a challenge in behalf of *Emmeline*, as *Gondibert*; and meet him, not as *Gondibert*, but *Emmeline*: I will take care to be prefent, not as *Elfrida* but *Edgar*: he will then be felf-convicted as a liar, by knowing neither of the perfons he has defam'd; and we may farther punifh him as we pleafe.

Emm. Well, I will try at this: but now difmifs me.   [*She breaks from his hand, and runs off.*

Edgar. Farewel, my love!---How has the hand of heav'n vouchfafed to guide me through all the mazes of my fate, to blifs! Even my revenge, my juftice
                                        rather,

rather, upon that wretch, whofe very folly is inve-
nom'd, fhall be compleat----But a mind fo bafe can
never be brave----Suppofe he fhould not come---He's
here.

Enter FLORIMOND. *Seeing* EDGAR, *he
ftops fhort.*

Flor. Gad take me---this damn'd madwoman is certainly fated to be my death.

[Edgar *advances towards him ; he draws back,
and looks frighted.*

Edgar. Sir, I am fo fhock'd when I reflect upon the
indecorums that my paffions have made me guilty of
to you, and my poor fpirits are fo flurried, that I really
am not able to make my 'pology.

Flor. Ma'am, I'm extreamly forry---and ma'am---
I muft abfolutely fly from your ladyfhip's apology.---
[*Going.*

Edgar. Sir, I muft beg the favour of your ear for
a few minutes---I hope, fir, you will pardon my con-
fufion---I have fomething to fay to you, fir, that---
Let me beg, fir, that you would come a little nearer---

Flor. (*afide.*) Pox on her--fhe wants to faften her
damn'd claws upon me again----(*To her*) Your commands, madam, always do me honour---And upon
my foul always leave me black and blue.   [*Afide.*

Edgar. I have juft heard, fir, fomething that has
fluftered me to fuch a degree---

Flor. (*afide.*) Aye---another fright ! fhe'll certainly
lay hold of me---(*retiring*) Ma'am---a, a, a, I hope
there's no danger threatens your ladyfhip.---

Edgar. Not directly me, fir ; nor indeed much
danger to you : but I was willing you fhould be
prepared—

Flor. Danger—prepared—for heav'n's fake, madam, what d' ye mean ?

Edgar.

Edgar. Why *Gondibert*, fir—you'll excufe my free-dom—Lard, that I fhould be fo indifcreet—I'm fen-fible, that the intereft I take in the affair, may be liable to conftructions of fuch a nature---that---

Flor. Lord, ma'am, if there is any villainous de-fign againft me, I befeech you to let me know it--- (*looking about.*) Perhaps we had better change our ground; fome villain may be taking aim at me as I ftand.

Edgar. You need not be under fuch apprehenfions, fir; it is a matter of no confequence—It is only, that *Gondibert* is to fend you a challenge, for the liberty you have taken with lady *Emmeline*; that's all---

Flor. Oh, if it's only an intention of *Gondibert* to cut my throat, to be fure that's a matter of no con-fequence---A bloody-minded ruffian! [*Afide.*

Edgar. Why, fir, to my certain knowledge, *Gondibert* knows no more of a fword, than a girl of eighteen; and has not a grain more courage.

Flor. (*taking courage*) Why, as to that, madam---

Edgar. As to that, fir, I am confident it would make no difference to you; but as I know he won't fight, and only prefumes upon an infolent opinion, that count *Florimond's* courage is as queftionable as his own—

Flor. (*bluftering.*) How, madam!

Edgar. Lard, fir, if you are fo violent, I fhall cer-tainly fall into my tremors---I fhall certainly want the fupport of your arm.

Flor. (*afide.*) Mercy upon me! and I fhall want but very little killing afterwards, if you do.

Edgar. I fay, fir, I think he fhould be properly expos'd; and I hope you'll act accordingly.

Flor. Madam—excufe me—a coward is my aver-fion; and you may depend upon his being chaftifed with moft exemplary feverity---but I fhould be forry to miftake his character (*afide*)---You know he won't fight?---

Edgar.

Edgar. (*a little haſtily*) Sir, if you ſuſpect my vera-
city---

Flor. O! Lord, madam---no, not in the leaſt.

Edgar. You'll excuſe me, ſir : I am really aſham'd
---of the liberty I have taken---Sir, your humble
ſervant.   [*Exit.*

Flor. Madam, your moſt obedient---Thank heav'n,
ſhe's gone---It was a lucid interval ; but it would not
have been of much longer continuance. I'm oblig'd
to her though, for her information----indeed am I----
Egad, I'll make a figure in this buſineſs---But if the
challenge is coming, I muſt be at home to receive
it.   [*Exit.*

S C E N E, *the dark Grove.*

Enter ſeveral Fairies.

1*ſt Fairy.* Come away, come away !
          We have jubilee to-day.
2*d Fairy.* Wherefore, wherefore ?
3*d Fairy.* Tell me.
4*th Fairy.* Tell me.
1*ſt Fairy.* E'er the ev'ning ſheds the dew,
          You ſhall know, and you, and you.
2*d Fairy.* What is finiſh'd ?
3*d Fairy.* What is plann'd ?
1*ſt Fairy.* Peace---the ſiſters are at hand.

Enter ELFINA *and* GROTILLA, *with
many Fairies in groteſque Characters.*

Elf. Now we triumph !---now 'tis paſt !
          Spells are broken, joy ſhall laſt !
          Let the voice of muſick riſe ;
          Muſic, grateful to the ſkies.

                                        A I R,

A I R, *with Chorus.*

We triumph, we triumph, with victory bleft ;
And beauty and truth are of pleafure poffefs'd.
Let mortals be told, and rejoice in the found,
" No lovers henceforward by fate fhall be-bound :"
There's now no conditions of pleafure but two,
Which they all may fulfil—to be tender *and* true.

Da Capo.

Elf. Now let ev'ry elf and fay
    Dance the laughing hours away :
    Let your nimble feet rebound,
    Lightly from the daified ground ;
    Trip it round, and round, and round.

[*A dance.*

Elf (stopping suddenly.) Hift—a mortal foot is nigh--
None muft here remain but I.

> [*Exeunt all but* Elfira, *who retires to the*
>   *back of the ftage.*

Enter F L O R I M O N D.

Flor. This is the place, and this is the time—but
I fee no figns of my little *Gondibertus*—Ha! here
comes a *bona roba*, whom I have not the honour to
know—Egad this affair will turn out with an eclat—
very much to my honour—I'll make the moft of it :
I'll let her into my bufinefs here, without feeming to
fee her.

> [Emmeline *enters in her own habit, and obferves*
>   *him ; he affects not to fee her ; but walks haftily*
>   *to and again, often looking on his watch, affect-*
>   *ing great impatience, and fpeaking as to himfelf.*

A poltron ! not to meet me upon his own challenge---
I'll make him know what it is to infult a man of ho-

F

nour

nour—If the wretch had met me, I would have given him his life ; but now to fpare him—a fcandal to mankind ! Ha ! (*affects to be furpris'd at feeing* Emmeline.) 'Death, interrupted and difcovered ! —-(*half afide.*) Madam—I proteſt—I am confounded—I am afraid that my natural impetuofity has a, a, a—

Emm. Sir, I am very forry that I fhou'd have intruded upon your privacy ; but, perhaps, I have prevented fomething that would have had worfe confequences.

Flor. Madam, I am not at liberty—

Emm. By the few words, fir, which juſt now involuntarily efcaped you, I know that you are waiting here upon an affair of honour—but I intreat—

Flor. Madam, it is impoffible—nothing but his life can atone for the infult.

Emm. You will excufe a woman, though a ſtranger, fir, upon fuch an occafion : may I intreat to know, fir, who has had the misfortune to incur the refentment of a gentleman, who feems fo little to deferve ill treatment, and fo able to punifh it ?

Flor. Madam, you do me honour---She is making advances already (*afide.*)---Why, madam, as the treatment I have received makes it an act of juſtice to tell, what I fhould otherwife rather die than difcover, I will comply with your requeſt---Hem ! A little dirty dependant upon the court here, madam, one *Gondibert*, thought fit to fend me a challenge, upon account of fomething I happened to fay concerning a lady, in whofe good graces I happen'd to be, and whom a foolifh young fellow that I was a friend to has thought fit to run away with ; and, madam, though I have fo far treated him like a gentleman, as to accept his challenge, he has not come to the place appointed, and it is now half an hour paſt the time.

Emm. (*looking out*) Methinks I fee fomebody at a diſtance, coming this way; perhaps that may be the gentleman—

Flor.

Flor. (*starting and looking out as afraid*) Ah! egad that's certainly he---(*aside.*) Now if he fhould not be a coward at laft---Madam a, a, a, for God's fake retire ---for---a, a, a.

Emm. Sir, I believe it will not be neceffary; for I'm pretty fure now, that the gentleman is a friend of mine---

Flor. A friend of yours, madam! pray who is he?

Emm. A gentleman, fir, who, l am fure, will be extreamly glad to be better known to you.

Enter EDGAR *in his proper drefs.*

Emm. (*afide.*) Yes, 'tis he, 'tis *Edgar!* With what elegance and dignity he looks the man!

Edgar. (*afide.*) How foft, how lovely in her female drefs!

Emm. (*to Florimond.*) Sir, as we are now no longer alone, I may confefs, that I am not altogether a ftranger to your perfon or your merit. (*To Edgar.*) Sir, this is *Florimond,* a gentleman to whom both you and I have fome obligations, which l believe he is not at prefent aware of.

Flor. Upon my word, madam, you abfolutely confound me---this exceffive honour---is it poffible that I fhould have been fo happy, as to confer obligations--- pray, madam, may I crave the honour of your name?

Edgar. Do you not at all recollect that lady, fir?

Flor. Upon my foul, fir, I cannot fay that l do.

Edgar. Who, now, do you think it can poffibly be, of all that your polite generofity has oblig'd?

Flor. Let me perifh, fir, if I can tell.

Edgar. Why, fir, that lady is one *Emmeline*; with whom, as fhe tells me, you was formerly moft intimately acquainted; and whom you lately converfed with, fir, in difguife, by the name of *Gondibert:* it's among ourfelves.---What! quite confounded, fir!

F 2

Flor.

Flor. (*recovering himself*) Ha! ha! ha! confounded! Ha! ha! ha! No, no, fir: you have had your jeft, and I have had mine. I knew well enough who I was talking to, when I play'd upon the little *Gondibertus*—Ah! I thought I fhould make you fmart for your frolic----I told *Elfrida* my whole fcheme----

Edgar. You told *Elfrida* your whole fcheme—

Emm. But pray, fir, as you did not know my perfon in my own drefs, how came you to know me in difguife?

Flor. Why, madam, to confefs the truth, I was let into the fecret by a friend. (*afide*) Egad, this goes fwimmingly.—

Edgar. Well, fir; but pray give me leave to bring you acquainted with a perfon, who, I'm fure, you are at prefent totally a ftranger to-----Pray, who do you think I am?

Flor. (*afide*) Heaven knows! but I wifh I was fairly out of your clutches—Upon my foul, fir, I have not the honour to know you, any otherwife than as a gentleman, whom I fhould be extremely proud to confider as my friend.

Edgar. Why, fir, I have the honour to be one *Edgar*; a very fhallow fellow, fir, that you had fome kindnefs for, becaufe he was aukwardly good-natured: I have alfo had the honour to receive feveral of your civilities, under the name of *Elfrida*------It's among ourfelves.

Flor. Sir, your moft humble fervant-----I have at this time fome urgent bufinefs-----

Edgar. So have I, fir; and therefore you muft not leave me yet----You may remember, fir, that you told me your whole fcheme to punifh *Emmeline* for her frolick, and to mortify her with ftories of herfelf by way of joke.

Flor. Sir, I befeech you ----

Edgar. Sir, I am extremely forry for the occafion; but as this lady has not got her fighting cloaths on,

you

you muſt excuſe me if I take her challenge upon my-ſelf; and ſo ſir---(*draws*)---it's among ourſelves.

Emm. What has my thoughtleſs indiſcretion done!

Flor. Ah, dear ſir, now you are too ſerious------

Emm. This muſt not be----For heav'ns ſake, *Edgar*, hear me!

Edgar. Fear not, my love---Sir, whatever you may think, this is but ſport to what is to follow---- and ſo, ſir, without more words----

Flor. O Lord, ſir!-----I beſeech you, madam——

Emm. For my ſake, *Edgar*——

Edgar. Truſt me—Draw, ſir, or——

Flor. Sir, I don't deſire to do you any harm; I don't, upon my ſoul, ſir.

Edgar. Scoundrel, coward, draw!

Emm. Conſider, *Edgar*—

Flor. Ay, do, dear ſir, conſider—

Edgar. Conſider what?

Flor. That I am but a poor, miſerable, lying cox-comb, ſir----Indeed, ſir, I am—

Emm. It is better to diſmiſs him, *Edgar*, as be-neath your reſentment.

Flor. So it is, indeed, ſir—a great deal better.

Emm. He is worthy only of contempt.

Flor. It is very true indeed, ſir,

Edgar. Art thou not a wretch, without the leaſt principle of truth or honour?

Flor. Yes, ſir.

Edgar. Art thou not infamous, as a ſlanderer and a coward?

Flor. Yes, ſir.

Edgar. Have not thy very follies the malignity of vices; and is it not a diſgrace to nature, to conſider thee as a man?

Flor. Any thing, dear ſir, if you will but ſpare my life.—If you chuſe any other ſatisfaction, ſir; if you would be content to kick me into ſome dark corner,

and

and leave me, I should think myself under infinite obligations to you.

Edgar. Hence then---and be thyself thy punishment !
[Florimond *runs off.*

As FLORIMOND *runs off,* ELFINA *comes forward.*

Ha !----Fear not, my *Emmeline* ! It is a friendly pow'r, familiar to my sight.

Emm. What ! is she known to you ?—My friend ! my guide !

Edgar. And mine !——(*both run and kneel to her.*)

Elf. Rise both, both blest !————

Emm. Forgive my diffidence—When my heart accused you, I was overwhelmed with distress !—Your promise to come at my call, was not fulfill'd.

Elf. I came not, that I might send you hither : (*pointing to Edgar*) Your friendship was the parent of your love.

Edgar. I too have need of your forgiveness ! pardon my distrust.

Elf. Say no more,—your fathers now
Ought to hear your mutual vow ;
Both the royal presence grace,
Heroes both of *British* race !
Go, your duties there present ;
I will answer for th' event.
Long may virtue guard your breast !
Joy shall then be long your guest.

[*The fairy disappears.*

Edgar. She's gone ! the kind propitious spright, that has led us, hoodwink'd, to the happiness, which, seeing, we had miss'd.

Emm. Let us then haste to follow her last advice ; for I can trust her now.

A

A FAIRY behind the scenes.

Edgar, Edgar, Edgar!
Emm. Hark! What voice?
Edgar. Perhaps some other kind and invisible be-
ing—There's music too—   [*An overture to a song.*

Emm. It comes, another tiny spright—It cannot
mean us ill—It beckons you—

RECITATIVE.

Fairy. Hear me, *Edgar* ; hear, and trust!
    Still be kind, and still be just :
    Truth and fondness that endure,
    Love from jealousy secure.

AIR.

Take and keep the fated fair,
Born to give supreme delight ;
Make her ever all thy care,
And secure thy envied right.

Clasp her to thy beating breast,
Round her lock thy faithful arms ;
These will guard her virtue best,
These will best secure her charms.
                        [*The fairy disappears.*

Edg. They need not such a guard, but yet shall have it.

Come then, my fair, whom Fate my love ordains,
By whom kind Heav'n o'erpays my fears and pains!
Chos'n as thou art for graces of the mind,
Ere gold could influence, or desire could blind ;
Whose charms, unsought, unknown, are friendship's
    dow'r ;
Whose love on reason founds its lasting pow'r.
O! might each pair thus work what Fate intends,
And none be lovers but who first were friends!

EPILOGUE.

Written by Mr. GARRICK.

Spoken by Mrs. YATES.

OLD times, old fashions, and the Fairies gone;
  Let us return, good folks, to sixty-one—
To this blest time, ye Fair, of female glory,
When pleasures unforbidden lie before ye!
No Sprites to fright you now, no guardian Elves;
Your wise directors are—your own dear selves—
And every Fair One feels, from old to young,
While these your guides——you never can do wrong.
Weak were the sex of yore—their pleasures few—
How much more wise, more spirited are You?
Would any Lady Jane, or Lady Mary,
Ere they did this or that, consult a Fairy?
Would they permit this saucy pigmy crew,
For each small slip, to pinch 'em black and blue?
Well may you shudder——for, with all your charms,
Were this the case—good heaven, what necks and arms!

  Thus did they serve our grandames heretofore——
The very thought must make us moderns sore!
Did their poor hearts for cards or dancing beat,
These Elves rais'd blisters on their hands and feet:
Tho' Loo the game, and fiddles play'd most sweetly—
They could not squeeze dear Pam, nor foot Moll Peatly.

Wer

EPILOGUE.

Were wives with husbands but a little wilful;
Were they at that same Loo *a little skilful;*
Did they with pretty fellows laugh or sport—
Wear ruffs too small, or petticoats too short:
Did they, no matter how, disturb their cloaths;
Or, over-lilied, add a little rose!—
These spiteful Fairies rattled round their beds,
And put strange frightful nonsense in their heads!
Nay, while the husband snor'd and prudish aunt,
Had the fond wife but met the dear gallant—
Tho' lock'd the door, and all as still as night—
Pop thro' the key-hole whips the Fairy Sprite,
Trips round the room—" My husband!" madam cries—
" The devil! where!" the frighted beau replies—
Jumps thro' the window—she calls out in vain—
He, cur'd of love—and cool'd with drenching rain,
Swears——" Dem him if he'll e'er intrigue again!"
These were their tricks of old——But all allow,
No childish fears disturb our Fair Ones now.——

Ladies, for all this trifling, 'twould be best
To keep a little Fairy *in your breast:*
Not one that should with moderate passions war;
But just to tweak you—when you go too far.

www.ingramcontent.com/pod-product-compliance
Lightning Source LLC
Chambersburg PA
CBHW021246260626
47172CB00002B/862